Blood of a Demon

Identity Unknown

Written by:

Nicole Donoho

PublishAmerica
Baltimore

ISBN: 1-4241-5359-X
PUBLISHED BY PUBLISHAMERICA, LLLP
www.publishamerica.com
Baltimore

Printed in the United States of America

Cover Art Designed by:
Fergi

Thank you for all your help with the cover.
Thank you more importantly for encouraging me
to dive deeper
into my imagination and swim awhile.
You truly are an inspiration and an
encouragement to me.
God knew that I needed you in my life at the
very moment you crossed my path.
Thanks for everything.
May He greatly expand your horizons with your
art career,
opening doors to unimaginable opportunities.
And bless you back for every way that you've
blessed me.

I'd like to dedicate this book to my parents.
Thank you for encouraging me to listen to God
and follow His plans.
Thank you for loving me and having patience
with me.
Thank you for encouraging me to dream big.
And most importantly, thank you for all the
ink and paper you bought for me.
This book is for you.

Special Thanks

To my husband, thank you for supporting me
and believing in me even when I didn't believe in
myself.
Thank you for always encouraging me.
I love you.

Too many people to name,
Not enough time to do.
To all of the people who helped me out,
To all the people who said, "Push through."
This is a very special thanks,
From me to all of you.

Thank you for being the best of friends,
Thank you for believing in me.
Thank you for supporting in every way,
And seeing what others didn't see.

You know who you are
You know what you said.
Because of your support
This book will be read.

Chapter 1

Chase watched the rain fall to the ground. It was the first rain that had fallen all month. Maybe that meant that today would go well. He felt a hand on his shoulder and quickly whipped around. "Whoa, watch what you're doing." Axel jumped back. "It's not a toy you know."

Chase looked down at the handgun. "I know."

"Are you going to be all right?"

"Yeah, I just don't want to talk right now."

"Chase..."

"Axel, I want to stay focused." Chase took a deep breath and looked out the window. It had been a long week. He was used to being busy and thrown into all types of craziness, but this week had been almost too much to handle.

"You don't have to be here. I can take you back to the house." Axel put his hand on Chase's shoulder again.

Chase jerked away. "Just stay the hell away from me, okay?"

The garage door on the warehouse opened and a primer black import pulled into the center. A small-framed, black-haired Asian man, with baggy black pants and tattooed arms, stepped out of the car, wearing a tattered gray backpack. Chase watched him walk up to the table that was set up in the center of the room. He watched as the guy unzipped the backpack to reveal the money inside and then looked out the window. The rain had stopped but everything still had a miserable murky gray color shadowing it.

Chase sighed and looked down at his watch. He had been through this routine more times than he could remember. Everything always went the same, with the few exceptions of some rambling drunk Russian or Chris Tucker wannabe who couldn't shut his mouth. Drug drops were always boring and always time consuming. This was life.

He was a Demon, a fourth generation Demon to be exact. His great-grandfather established the Black Demons almost seventy years ago. He died in a gang shoot-out leaving Chase's grandfather, Victor Laney as his successor. Victor suffered a massive heart attack three days after Chase was born. Miraculously, he recovered fully in just a few months. The heart attack made Victor realize that time could be taken away from him at any given moment; and so he passed on leadership of the Black Demons to his son David Laney.

Chase became a Black Demon before he could walk or talk. It wasn't a choice; it was in his blood. His dad raised him as a Demon and never gave him the option for anything else. He learned how to shoot a gun when he was four. He was a perfect shot by the time he was five. His mom tried to encourage him in other things—sports, books, video games—anything to keep him away from the Demons. Despite her efforts, Chase followed in the footsteps of his father and earned his colors when he was sixteen. He was marked a Black Demon for life.

Chase looked down at the tattoo on the inside of his wrist. He could still remember the adrenaline rush he experienced the day he earned it. It was a stupid mission that seemed childish now, but then it was his first step to be part of the gang. He had to hold up a gas station, wait for the cops to show up and then get away from the cops.

Since that day, everything had become a series of repeated events. During the week he would sell drugs for his dad and on the weekends he would party with Axel. There wasn't much else to do. He was a Demon; the only thing he could do was everything his dad instructed him.

"Do you want to go down to the club and pick up Sarah? That will get you in a better mood."

"I don't know."

Axel sighed. "Chase, you have to stop thinking about it. There wasn't anything else you could have done."

"Deal's closed," a voice announced over Chase's cell phone.

Chase walked over to the table and grabbed the briefcases from Axel's dad, Xavier. "Are you feeling okay?"

"Yes."

"Axel, maybe you should take Chase back to the house and I'll take the money down to the..."

"I said I'm feeling fine!" Chase threw the briefcases in the trunk and looked at the other guys in the warehouse. "If one more person decides I need a psychiatrist I swear I'll shoot you and the person next to you," Chase yelled.

"Chase?" Xavier stepped towards him and Chase drew his gun.

"Don't push me, Xavier." Chase looked at the other guys in the warehouse. They had their hands on their guns but their eyes were jumping from Xavier to Chase. Chase lowered his gun and opened the car door. "Axel, get in the car."

Axel walked around to the driver's side. He got into the car. "Chase, what the hell are you doing? Have you lost it? You just pulled a gun on my dad. You're lucky the whole warehouse didn't erupt in gunfire."

Chase covered his face with his hands. "I don't know."

"You don't know what? How stupid that was or why you did it?"

"I don't know." Chase sighed and rested his head on the back of the seat. "I'm not even sure who I am anymore."

Axel was the only person Chase could confide in about anything. He was a second generation Demon and sixteen years older but he was also Chase's bodyguard. They had been together since Chase was born and Chase always thought of him more as a brother than a bodyguard.

Axel backed out of the warehouse. In all his years of watching over him, Chase had never been one to show a lot of emotion. After the past week, everything about him had changed including his appearance. Axel glanced at Chase; his usually darkly tanned skin was pale and his brown eyes were red and puffy from lack of sleep. "Listen, Chase, shit happens and there's nothing you can do about it. If you don't push this aside and get on with your life…I'm afraid you won't have one. You have to let it go."

Let it go? Chase looked out the window and rubbed his eyes to stop the tears that were forming. How was he supposed to let this go? The images of his mother's swollen face would be burned into his memory for the rest of his life. His dad told him that he had to go to the funeral so he could "get closure." Whatever that meant, it sure wasn't helping. Chase felt worse after seeing his mom lying there in the coffin. She'd never open her eyes again. "She didn't deserve that."

"Nobody deserves that. Your mom was just in the wrong place at the wrong time. There isn't anything that anyone could have done, Chase."

"It's my fault. I should have…"

"Dragons, we got Dragons coming up fast from the south," a voice announced over the phone.

A black import slid out of an alley in front of them and gunfire rained down on the car. Axel turned down an alley. "They're coming from the north too," he yelled into the cell phone.

"It was a set-up," Xavier yelled. "I want everyone out of here now!"

Chase leaned out the window and fired a few rounds. He dropped back into his seat as Axel whipped the car down another alley. "Axel, we've got to get…" A bullet hit the back window and shattered glass sprayed onto the backseat. "Axel!"

"I'm working on it, Chase." He slid onto the pier at the end of the alley.

Chase looked out his window at the ocean below. "I think you need to work a little harder on that plan, buddy."

"Shut up!"

"Well, get us off this freakin' pier!" Chase yelled.

Chase saw an import out of the corner of his eye and turned just as the import slammed into Axel's door. The back of his head slammed into the window and everything disappeared into darkness.

Axel watched the pier disappear above him. Cold water surged in through the back window and slammed his body forward into the steering wheel. He reached for Chase as the car sank to the ocean floor.

***

Chapter 2

"Jesse, I only have three weeks. Can we please go?" Cali did her best to make a pathetically sad face.

"I never should have sat you on a surfboard."

Cali smiled. "It's a little late for that."

Jesse walked into his bedroom. "I thought it was raining out?"

"What does a little rain matter when you're going to get wet anyway?" Cali looked out the window. The rain had stopped for now but it was still cloudy.

Jesse walked out of the room. "Well, let's go. If we're going to surf then I want to go now."

Cali grabbed her surfboard off the coffee table and followed Jesse outside. Jesse looked back at Cali. Her wavy sun-kissed hair was pulled back into a messy bun. Her eyes were shining and you could almost see the energy pulsating from her lightly tanned skin. She definitely looked out of place against the cloudy gray horizon. "Aren't you even the least bit tired?"

"No, why do you ask?"

"Um, maybe because you just flew halfway around the world."

She smiled. "What can I say? I was born to travel."

Jesse shook his head. "You know, I'm still surprised that your parents let you come."

Cali laughed. She was an only child, which usually meant that she was by her parents' side twenty-four/ seven. There was never any other family around to watch her and she was always too young to travel alone, at least in her dad's eyes. "Well, Dad told me to do what God was telling me to do."

"Well, I guess He knows something about something since He told you to come here."

"No offense, but I don't think he brought me here for the scenery." Cali waded out. "He did a much better job on Australia."

Jesse waded out behind her. "I'm insulted, I really am." Cali laughed. "No, I'm serious, Cali, you should find a nice place on the beach to sleep for the next three weeks."

Cali laughed and shook her head. "Okay."

"I guess I better not threaten you with sleeping outside. Your dad told me about the hammock."

"Have you ever slept in a hammock?"

Jesse laughed. "Actually, your dad and I set up some hammocks under the pier when we were teenagers. We used to sneak out of the house with our boards and sleep under there so we could claim the best spots in the morning."

"Did you do it a lot?"

"Well, Bob made us honorary citizens."

"Who's Bob?"

"He was the crazy homeless guy that lived under the pier." Jesse laughed.

Cali stopped and sat up. "Jesse, have you ever thought about moving?"

"This is my home; where else would I go?"

"You could come to Australia."

Jesse sighed. He missed being able to hang out with Cali's dad. They had been inseparable best friends since Jesse was two and he was five. So much so, that everyone in school including most of the teachers thought that they were brothers. "My life's here, Cal. What would I do with the Surf Shack if I left?"

She shrugged. "Sell it."

"Bite your tongue, little girl," Jesse said with a surfer twang, "If the surf gods hear that talk there'll be hell to pay."

Cali laughed. The thought of living in the same city for thirty years seemed strange. She had never lived in the same country for more than two years and never lived in the same city more than a year. That was the luxury of being the daughter of missionaries. Traveling all over the world might seem like a fun adventure to some people or maybe a luxurious vacation, but to Cali it was as common as going to the bathroom.

When she was six, her parents came back to the

states to raise money for a church they had started in Mali, Africa. During those four months, she stayed with Jesse. He taught her how to surf and she loved it. Now that her parents lived in Australia she had plenty of time to work on her surfing. It was her getaway from all the craziness of life.

Cali took out her bun and let her hair drop down on her shoulders. She looked at the pier and then glanced at Jesse. "I'll race you to it."

"Okay, but you're going to lose." Jesse dropped down on his board and paddle furiously.

There was no doubt that Jesse would win; he was born on the water. Cali always joked that he could surf better than he could walk, which was proven true after his many run-ins with trash cans and benches. No matter how hard Cali paddled Jesse stayed ten feet in front of her, until he stopped and sat up on his board. Cali stopped by him. "Don't tell me you're quitting."

"No." Jesse pointed to two cars speeding down the pier. Another car came out of an alley and slammed into the car in the front. It shattered the rails on the pier and spiraled to the ocean below. Jesse dropped down wildly paddling to the shore. A dark-haired guy popped out of the water gasping for air. "Is anyone else down there?"

The man nodded as he choked up water. He held up one finger. "Just one?" He nodded again. Jesse unsnapped his board and dove into the water.

Cali quickly grabbed the board and pushed it over

to the man bobbing in the water. He put his arms on the board. He looked like he was in his late twenties. Cali paddled up next to him and helped him onto the board. "I should go help him."

"Jesse's a certified lifeguard and scuba diver; he'll be okay. Are you hurting anywhere?"

"No."

Axel lay back on the surfboard and took a deep breath. He was alive, for now. David's money was sitting in a car at least thirty-five feet under the ocean. He was alive, for now.

Jesse felt the salt burning his eyes as he swam deeper. He saw the car and swam in through the hole that used to be the back window. He wrapped his arms around the body and pulled it over the seats to the back window. He tried pulling it out of the back window and it got caught on something. He pushed the bag away from the body and kicked furiously for the surface.

Cali was already off her board when he burst through the surface. "Hand me your board," Jesse yelled. He grabbed the board and pushed the body halfway onto the board to push it to shore. He got to the shore and the other guy helped him pull the body onto the sand. Jesse felt for a pulse. "He's still alive!"

Cali watched Jesse push on the guy's chest. He looked like he was around her age. His skin was pale and blood was spilling out of the left side of his forehead. Cali unzipped her wetsuit and pressed it against his head. *God, please don't let him die. There's so much more he can do.*

He choked up water and Jesse helped him sit up. "Chase?" The other guy dropped down to his knees. "What hurts? Does anything hurt?"

Chase could hear muffled voices and see scrambled images in front of him. There were people in front of him, five, no three sitting in front of him. He pushed himself up and felt the blood rush to his head. He swayed and then dropped down on one of the images. The person came into focus. It was a girl, a drop-dead gorgeous girl with wavy blonde hair flung wildly on the sand below her. Her eyes were intense; a blue so bright it put tropical waters to shame. A drop of red hit her face.

Chase pushed himself up and touched the red spot. "I blood your thinking." She looked at him with confusion. Chase took a deep breath to pull his thoughts into words. "I think you're bleeding."

"No, actually you are." She picked up a wetsuit and pushed it to his forehead. He jerked back. "The salt water will burn but you have to keep pressure on it."

Chase lay back in the sand and let her hold the wetsuit tight against his head. Axel knelt down next to them. "Are you all right?"

"I think so."

"I'm going to find a payphone and…"

"I have a shop just up the beach. You can go there

with me and we can bring my jeep back to pick him up." Jesse looked at Cali. "Are you okay?"

Jesse picked up the surfboards. "It's about half a mile. Do you think you can make it?" Axel nodded.

Chase looked at Cali. Her bright blue bikini matched her eyes and looked perfect on her tan skin. "Do you live around her?"

Chase was a bit thrown off by her question. He was still enjoying the sweetness of the eye candy that was sitting next to him. "What?"

"Do you live around here?"

"Ah, no, I live on the other side of town."

"What's your name?"

"Chase."

"Do you..."

"Listen..."

"Cali."

"Right, listen, Cali, I'm not really in the mood for small talk. I'm sure you're in shock right now and I understand but my head feels like someone slammed a hammer into it so I'm not in the mood to listen to whatever shit you're going to ramble about."

"In shock?" Cali looked at him with confusion.

"Yeah, a little surfer girl like yourself probably isn't used to seeing a body pulled from a car that just dove off the pier."

"A little surfer girl like me?" Cali smiled. "I've seen worse."

Chase laughed. There was no way this girl could have seen anything worse than what she'd seen today. "You look way too innocent to have seen anything worse than this."

"And flying off a pier is normal for you?"

"No, this is the first time I've been driven off a pier but I am used to craziness."

"Craziness?" Cali smiled; she knew a lot about craziness. "You mean, like gunshots echoing through your house and people dropping down dead in your front yard?"

Chase looked at her with confusion. "Where are you from?"

"I'm from too many places to name." She pulled the wetsuit off Chase's head and sat back.

She had a knock-out body and an attitude. She was a life-size pin-up girl, come to make his world a better place. "Do you live around here?"

"No, I'm just visiting."

"Who was that old guy?"

"Old guy?" Cali cocked her eyebrow and laughed. "You mean, Jesse?"

"Yeah, he's not your boyfriend or something is he?"

Cali stared at Chase. She never had a guy hit on her before but she was pretty sure Chase was. "No, he's more like my uncle only not related."

"Maybe I could take you out sometime then."

She laughed. "I don't think so."

"Why?"

"I think you hit your head a little too hard."

"What? Why do you say that?"

"Um, well, you're trying to hook up with a girl you don't even know and for some reason...you think that she might be interested."

***

Axel followed Jesse into the building. Jesse turned on the lights which seemed to illuminate surfboard heaven. Surfboards stood like soldiers along each wall and formed aisles in the middle of the floor. "What is this place?"

"Welcome to Surf Shack. You can consider yourself a VIP; we're usually closed on Sundays." Jesse pointed to the counter. "The phone's on the shelf below the counter."

Axel walked over to the counter and dialed the phone.

"Hello?"

Axel recognized his brother's voice. "Ayden, it's me."

"Axel, where are you guys? We've been calling your phones for the past hour."

Axel shook the water from his cell phone. "Well, our service is a little diluted right now."

"What happened? Are you two okay?"

"Yeah, I'll tell you about it later." Axel watched Jesse walk into another room. "Listen, I need you to pick me up. We're down by the pier."

"The pier?"

"Ayden, I don't have time to talk about it."

"All right, what are you around?"

"It's this place called Surf something."

"Surf what?"

"Hey!" Axel yelled. Jesse walked out of the other room and shut the door. "Where are we at?"

"Surf Shack, it's off of Hammond Road."

"It's called Surf Shack," Axel repeated into the receiver. "It's off of Hammond Road."

"Okay, I'll be there in about thirty minutes."

"All right, bye." He hung up the phone and looked at Jesse. "My brother's coming to pick us up."

"I could have taken you home."

"Well, we have to stop by the police station and file a report," Axel lied. "That will probably take some time."

"Oh, you're right, I completely forgot about that." Jesse grabbed his keys off the wall. "If you need me or Cali to come in and give a statement just let us know."

"I don't think it will be necessary. I got a pretty good look at the car when it hit us."

***

Cali stared at Chase. She couldn't believe how straightforward he was. "Sorry, but I'm not interested in a date."

"What about dinner?" There was something that Chase couldn't let go of with this girl. Maybe he had hit his head too hard but he couldn't stop staring at her.

She was relieved when she saw Jesse coming in the jeep. The conversation would finally end. "No, thanks."

***

Chase crawled into the back of Ayden's Navigator. His head was throbbing with pain. He leaned his seat back and watched Cali walk into the Surf Shack with Jesse. He would definitely have to come back to see her again.

"So what happened?" Ayden asked.

"Some Dragons came out of an alley and rammed us off the pier." Axel leaned his seat back. "My body feels like someone ran me through a meat grinder."

"You're lucky those surfers were out there. Do you think they were suspicious of anything?"

"Our car flew off the pier and we were still alive. They didn't really question us, Ayden."

"Well, David's not too happy. He thinks you guys should have been a little more careful."

"A little more careful?" Chase objected and looked at Ayden. "They slammed into us and knocked us off the pier. How is he turning this into being our fault?"

Axel sighed. "I never should have got onto the pier in the first place."

"No, no!" Chase yelled. "This is not your fault, Axel. My dad set up the drop so it's his fault the Dragons ambushed us."

"Chase…"

"Stop sticking up for him!" Chase yelled. His head was throbbing and he felt like he would pass out any minute but this was an argument he couldn't back down from. "I'm sick of everyone sticking up for him and running to his every request. He doesn't give a shit about anybody else so why should we give a shit about him?"

"Chase, he takes responsibility for what he does," Ayden objected.

"Yeah, like he took responsibility for Mom's death? He sent her on that errand knowing full well that she didn't have anybody with her."

"He couldn't have known that store would get held up, Chase."

"He should have ran the freakin' errand himself or even went with her but he didn't. He made her go like he always does, like she was just another one of his hookers that he orders around."

"Chase…"

"Just shut up! I don't want to hear any more." Chase stared out the window. The throbbing in his temples increased the more he fought back tears. "Drop me off at Grandpa's house."

"Chase, David said that he wanted you to…"

"Screw what David said, Ayden. Take me to my Grandpa's house." David was the last person he wanted to be around. He was the reason his life was miserable.

***

Chapter 3

Cali walked into the dark room. "Hello? Hello is anybody there?" It seemed like nothing was in the room except totally darkness. The kind you look into in the middle of the night before your eyes adjust to the little bits of light around you. Something passed by her arm and she jumped. "Who's there?"

She lifted up the light to get a better look at what was in the room. Even with the lamp she was holding, the room still seemed to be unusually black. She saw something move again and walked towards it. "Hello? Is someone there?"

She scanned her lamp across the room in front of her until she came across something. A dark silhouette was leaning over a body on the ground. She ran over to see what was wrong and the silhouette disappeared once her light hit it. The person was still lying on the ground with his hands by his neck. Cali stopped. It was Chase. She knelt down by him to see what was wrong. "Help," he gasped and held tight to something wrapped around his neck.

Cali reached down to help him pull off whatever was choking him. There was nothing on his neck. "Hang on. I'll try to find help."

"No," Chase gasped. "Don't leave me." Chase disappeared.

Cali sat up and took a deep breath. Her body was covered in sweat but she was shivering. It was a dream. She looked around the room. Nothing seemed to be out of place.

Jesse burst into the room. "Are you okay?" She nodded. "I heard you screaming; what happened?"

Cali shook her head. She was still trying to figure out the dream. Still trying to convince herself that she had now returned to reality. She grabbed Jesse's arms and buried her head against his chest. Jesse wrapped his arms around her. She could hear his heart beating beneath his t-shirt. He was real; he wasn't a dream.

***

"I think it would be good for you to step back from everything."

"You know I can't do that." Chase sighed and grabbed a beer from the fridge.

"Chase, I know the Demons' rules. Shit, I made most of them." His grandpa pointed to the chair across from him. "I also know what's going through your head right now, but you can't do this to yourself."

"What am I supposed to do? I don't have anything else to do. I don't even know anything else to do."

"What about your music? You're always messing with that guitar of yours."

"It's just for fun, Grandpa; it's not like there's anyway I can make a career out of it. Besides, who would hire me with my record?"

"That's why you need to step away from it."

"I can't get out of it. As much as I hate it, the Black Demons are my life."

"Chase, listen to someone who has been there. If you stay with the Demons, you won't have a life."

"I've got nothing to walk away to."

"Freedom, that's what you have to walk away to." His grandpa leaned back in his chair and lit his cigar. "Look at me, what do I have? I have a big empty house to myself. I gave everything that I had to the Demons. Most of those guys started out younger than you and I raised them up to what they are now. Do you see any of them around here?"

"Yeah, but you had to walk away."

"I chose to walk away, Chase. And I chose to put your dad in charge, which is a decision I've had to live with every day since."

***

Sarah stood next to the table. "Can you make this quick? I have to be back on stage in ten minutes."

Chase looked at Sarah. Her breasts were almost falling out of her bra which wouldn't make any difference after she got onto stage. "Sit down." Sarah sat down across from him. Chase had been going out with her for almost two years now. He was the one that hired her for his dad's club. "I'm thinking about leaving the Demons."

Sarah pulled back and looked at him with confusion. "Why?"

"I just need to get away and figure things out. I was thinking about taking a trip somewhere, maybe to Mexico."

"So, why are you telling me this?"

"I was hoping that you'd come with me."

"Sarah, you're on in three," someone yelled.

"I can't."

Chase shook his head in shock. "What do you mean you can't?"

"I can't leave, Chase. I have a really good job and I don't want to take a break."

"I can talk to my dad and have him work out your pay so you can…"

"I don't want to go. I think it would be better if you just went by yourself."

"Are you breaking up with me?" Chase looked at her with confusion.

She nodded. "I don't think it's going to work out anymore." She got up and kissed his check. "I have to get on stage but have fun in Mexico."

Chase took a deep breath. That did not go as planned. He thought for sure that Sarah would be all for going to Mexico. He grabbed his jacket and walked out the back door.

***

"Oh, stop there, Jesse!" Jesse jerked the jeep into the gas station and looked at Cali with confusion. "I forgot to get some water. I don't want to be down there all day with nothing to drink."

Jesse handed her a ten dollar bill. "Okay, hurry."

Cali ran into the gas station. When Jesse found out she was coming, he volunteered her to paint the nursery at his church. They wanted Noah's Ark and all the animals to wrap around the entire room. Cali had yet to see the room but from Jesse's description, she would have her work cut out for her during the next three weeks.

She grabbed two bottles of water and walked up to the line by the counter. "Cali?"

Cali turned around, surprised that anyone would know her name. Chase was standing in the candy aisle. He walked up to her. "This is really weird running into you here."

Cali smiled. *You have no idea.* "Yeah, it is."

"I can't remember if I ever really thanked you for pulling me out of that car." Chase tightened his grip on the bags of chips he was holding. "I can't remember if I said anything that day to tell you the truth."

Cali shrugged. "Your brain was pretty scrambled; I won't hold it against you." She looked down at the bags of chips and boxes of cookies he was holding. "Going on a trip?"

Chase looked at her with confusion. "Actually, yeah, I was thinking about taking a vacation. How did you know?"

She pointed to his snacks. "I'm used to stocking up. Where are you going?"

"I'm thinking about Mexico."

"I would definitely reconsider the chocolate cookies then, if I was you. I took some on a trip to Africa and after about two days I had chocolate syrup and soggy cookies. It was not a pretty sight."

"Africa? That's pretty far. Was that like a safari or something?"

"Actually, it was a mission trip. We spent the week traveling to villages in the area telling them about God." Cali looked at the counter; she was next in line. The image of Chase choking popped into her head. *God, I can't tell him about the dream. I don't even know who he is.* She sighed. There was no way getting around what had to be done; she just wasn't sure how to do it. She looked at Chase. He was looking through his snacks. "Are you leaving soon?"

"I'm thinking about leaving tomorrow. I was hoping that there wouldn't be as much traffic if I left on a weekday. It's kind of an off day and nobody usually travels on it." Cali smiled. Chase took a deep breath and looked down at the snacks in his arms. Her smile was so intense and yet, it was just a smile. *What is your deal, Chase? You've had thousands of girls smile at you.* Chase looked at Cali. There was no smile that could compare to the intensity and innocence of that smile. He looked down at his bag and tried to look like he was taking an inventory.

"This is going to sound really strange and I don't want you to get the wrong idea but..." Chase looked up at Cali. The smile had been replaced with a nervous look. What did she have to be nervous about? "Do you think that you would want to get something to eat? Like for lunch or something?"

Chase stared at her for a moment. Maybe she wasn't as innocent as she appeared to be. "I don't know."

"You don't know?" Cali seemed to regain her confidence. "Two days ago you're asking me out and now you don't know about having lunch?"

"I was in shock. I almost died and then this gorgeous girl is..." Chase lost all train of thought when she broke out her smile again. How could he say no to this girl? Her bright blue eyes, her perfect lips, and trim body—it was like she popped out of a magazine just for him to fully enjoy her.

"How 'bout surfing?" Cali said quickly.

"What?"

"Surfing, do you know how?"

Chase laughed. Surfing was the last thing on his to-do list. "No, I don't know how to surf."

"How can you go to Mexico and not know how to surf?"

"There's others things you can do." Chase smiled as he thought about girls walking down the beach in G-strings.

"All right, here's the thing. I'm sorry about shutting you down the other day. I had just got here and I wasn't ready for some guy to hit on me." *Not that I'd ever be ready for that.* "Anyways, I don't want you to get the wrong impressions and think that suddenly I am interested; it's just that I've felt really bad since then."

Chase laughed. "Oh, you want to take me out to clear your conscious then."

"If that is the way you want to put it, then yes."

"Don't worry about it."

Cali sighed and faced the counter. *Okay, God, I tried. If I'm supposed to help him then you have got to do something.*

Chase looked at Cali and smiled. She felt guilty? It was kind of funny. He glanced down; her shorts came down longer than most girls he knew but they were still tight enough to show off her amazing curves. What could be the worst thing that could happen from hanging out with this girl for a couple hours? He wanted a distraction from the Demons and here was a five-foot distraction that would definitely keep his mind off the Demons. "Is it really that hard to surf?"

Cali turned around. "Does that mean you're interested in trying?"

Chase shrugged. "I guess I don't have anything better to do this afternoon and if it will help to make you feel better than I guess I've done my good deed." *Who knows, maybe I'll get a little booty out of it.*

***

Chapter 4

"Are you sure about this, Cali?" Jesse looked out the window at Chase. He was sitting on his motorcycle with his feet propped up between the handlebars.

"Jesse, there's something he needs help with." Cali zipped her wetsuit shut and grabbed a surfboard.

"Cali, you barely even know him." Jesse walked over to the counter. "Did you stop think that maybe you're reading too far into this dream?"

"I'm not," Cali objected. "I seen Chase on the floor and he was choking. There's something that's smothering him, Jesse, something that he can't get away from."

Jesse pulled down the blinds again. "Maybe whatever is smothering him has cut off the circulation to his brain for quite some time."

"What?"

"He's riding a crotch rocket without a helmet."

"And?"

"Cali, that's one of the fastest on the market. People don't buy them to drive behind grandmas." Cali laughed. Jesse was pacing behind the counter like her dad always did when he was about to make a big decision. "I don't think you should go with him."

"Why?"

"Why?" Jesse slammed his hands down on the counter. "You did not just ask me that question. Your parents are trusting me to keep you out of trouble so there's no way that I can let you go surfing with a hormone-possessed motorcycle freak. I can't do it."

"Jesse," Cali laughed, "would you listen to yourself? That's probably what parents said about you and my dad when you were younger."

"When I was younger..."

Cali grabbed his face with her hand. "Jesse, I'm a big girl."

"No, you're not," Jesse said through his squeezed lips. "You're innocent and you don't know anything about American boys."

Cali let go of his face. "Jesse, we're going to be right out on the beach. If you're worried about me you can sit outside and watch everything."

"I don't want to be like a hovering father."

"You won't, you'll be like the hip uncle that likes to tan."

"You think this is a joke don't you?" Jesse grabbed a beach chair. "I'm serious. I don't care how old you are. You're not getting mixed up with a boy on my watch; oh no, your dad is not holding that over my head."

Cali smiled. "That's great, Jesse; you should call God and tell him to give my angel the day off." Cali walked outside. Chase put his legs down. She looked at his jeans. "You're not going to surf in those are you?"

Chase looked down at his jeans. "I could surf in my boxers if you'd like that better."

Cali could feel her face blushing. "No that's okay. Why don't you go inside and get a wetsuit from Jesse. He just got a new shipment in."

Chase got off the motorcycle and walked into the Surf Shack. Jesse was pulling a beach chair out from behind the counter. "If there's anything I can..." He turned around and stopped when he saw Chase. "Yes?"

"Cali said I should get a wetsuit from you."

"You didn't bring one?"

Chase shook his head. "I'm not really into surfing on a regular basis. I tried telling Cali that I could just surf in my boxer but..."

"Let's find you a wetsuit; what size do you wear?" Jesse said quickly. "Medium? Large? Let's try a medium-large and go from there." Jesse quickly grabbed a wetsuit off the rack and handed it to Chase.

Chase looked at the full body wetsuit. "How 'bout something where the legs are a little shorter like Cali's maybe."

Jesse looked out at Cali. "Well, Cali doesn't know much about surfing, just enough to get her by. I keep telling her that she needs to wear a wetsuit with longer legs to help...to keep the pressure down when she...falls...if she falls off the board."

Chase cocked his eyebrow. He had seen this stumbling before. It was how Axel acted every time Samantha caught him in a lie. "Is there something wrong?"

Jesse took a deep breath. "No, why do you ask?"

Chase shook his head. He took the wetsuit from Jesse. "Don't I need to wear some trunks under this?"

"Yeah, definitely." Jesse pointed to a rack next to a room. "You can take any of those. The changing rooms are over there."

***

"This is punishment isn't it? Since I don't have any kids I'm getting repaid through Troy's aren't I?"

Cali laughed. "Jesse, calm down, it's not like he's taking me on a date; we're just surfing."

"Yeah, that's what your dad and I told our moms right before we..." Jesse stopped. "Well, let's just say surfing wasn't the only thing we did at the beach."

"Too much information!" Cali yelled.

Jesse took her hands off her ears. "Listen to me, Cali. Boys only have one thing on their mind and it's not surfing. I should know. I was one once."

"You were once a boy? What are you now?" Cali giggled; she couldn't help it. He had set himself up for that one.

"Cali, you know what I mean."

"Jesse, you're being ridiculous."

"No, I'm not; I'm serious. I know how they think because I was young and I thought the same way."

"You were different and the girls you hung out with didn't have values and standards."

"Hey now!"

"What?" Cali smiled. "I know what kind of girls you guys hung out with before my dad met my mom. You need to lighten up. I didn't invite him to the dark corners under the pier." Cali spun around. "I invited him to surf on an open beach. Have a little faith in me. I'm not underestimating the power of 'raging hormones.'"

Chase looked at himself in the mirror and laughed. "God, if Axel was here he'd be laughing his ass off."

He walked outside and set his clothes on top of his motorcycle. Cali was down by the beach pushing sand into a pile and Jesse was setting up his beach chair a couple feet away. Chase walked up to Cali. "What are you building, a sandcastle?"

Cali smiled. "No." She packed down the sand and set a surfboard on top of it. "Go ahead and get on."

"What?"

"First, you learn here and then you take it out there."

"If the zipper's broke on that one I can get you another one." Jesse yelled.

Chase looked down at the top of the wetsuit hanging below his waist. "No, I'm fine."

Cali looked at Chase. His stomach was chiseled with the perfect six pack and the muscles in his arms were bulging. Every piece seemed to be accented with a different tattoo. Chase lay down on the board showing off three more tattoos on his back. Cali was most intrigued by the one on left shoulder; it was four-inch heart made out of barbed wire with the name "Julia" written in the middle of it. She could tell by how bright the ink was that it had to have been done recently. "Who is Julia?"

Chase glanced back at Cali. "What?"

"This tattoo." Cali tapped his shoulder. "Who is Julia, if you don't mind me asking?"

"Julia was my mother. She died ten days ago."

"Oh, I'm sorry."

"It's not your fault." Chase shook his head. He didn't want to get into a pity party and he didn't want to talk about his mom. "Are we going to do this surf lesson or what?"

"Yeah." Cali sat down next to the surfboard. "Okay first you're going to lie flat on your board."

Jesse watched Cali giving Chase instruction. He hadn't liked her hanging out with Chase before and now that his shirt was off he really didn't want her by him. "The boy spent more time decorating his body than I spent decorating my entire house," Jesse mumbled under his breath. His cell phone rang. "Hello?" He didn't get much from the broken-up call. "Hold on, I'm down on the beach; let me walk up to the house where I can get a better signal."

***

Cali pulled the zipper up on the back of Chase's wetsuit. "If you're going to surf, you're going to have to get used to that."

"Who puts a zipper in the back?" Chase objected and lay down on the board. "I mean, I can understand on the back of a girl's wetsuit because girls are used to having zipper in the back, but on a guy's? What guy has a jacket that zips up backwards?"

Cali smiled. "You'll have to ask Jesse about the reasoning for that. He's the one that has the answers to surf questions."

"Yeah, I don't think Jesse likes me very much."

"Why do you say that?"

Chase shrugged. "Just the way he acts. He told me that you don't surf very much."

"Jesse told you that?" Cali shook her head. As if one over-protective father wasn't bad enough. "I live in Australia. I go surfing almost every day. I hold services on the beach with the surfers every Sunday morning before we go surfing."

"First Africa, now Australia?" Chase sat up on the board. "Any other countries you've visited?"

"Actually, Africa's a continent divided into small countries." Cali looked at the shore. "I've been to quite a few. My parents are missionaries and they take me on all their trips, well except for this one."

"Missionaries?" *You know how to pick them, Chase!*

"They're people that…"

"I know what missionaries are. My grandma's church would send them down to Mexico all the time. I'm just surprised that you're one."

"Surprised that I'm one?"

"Yeah, most of missionaries at my grandma's church are women whose hairdos are older than most dead people."

"What church does your grandma go to?" Cali laughed.

"She went to one down the street from my house. She died a while back."

"Do you go to church?"

Chase couldn't help but laugh. "Do I look like someone that goes to church?"

"Whoever said you had to look a certain way to go to church?"

"A lot of people."

"Well, you don't."

"I'm not really in to the whole church thing. The last time I went to church was for my mom's funeral and before that for my grandma's." Chase looked down at the surfboard. "So, how do you work this thing?"

"Wait for a swell to come, paddle as hard as you can, and stand up when it breaks into a wave."

"And I'm sure it's not as simple as you're making it out to be."

"Sure it is." Cali looked at the swell coming. "Okay, turn around and start paddling."

Chase turned around and paddled next to Cali. Cali was paddling ahead of him. He jumped up as soon as she jumped up which proved to be a huge mistake. The board slipped out from underneath him and he found himself struggling to find the surface inside the wave.

Cali sat down on her board and watched for Chase to surface. He burst out of the water and reached for his board. Cali paddled up next to him. He was choking up water. "Are you okay?" He nodded. "Don't expect to get it on the first time."

"I wasn't expecting to but I was I wasn't expecting to swallow half the ocean."

"Here, let me take me board in and I'll be right back."

Chase watched Cali lay her board in the sand and then swim back out. He was actually beginning to have fun. He could look like an idiot and no one was around to laugh about it. "Have you decided I'm hopeless?"

"No," Cali smiled, "I decided you could use more help."

Cali pulled herself onto the board and then helped Chase up. "The benefits of a using a long board is you can have two people. I'll sit to keep the board's balance and you stand up."

"Here? But there aren't any waves."

"It will help you get the feel of standing up. Give me the cord so you don't get tangled up." Chase unsnapped the cord around his ankle and handed it to Cali. He grabbed the sides of the board and slowly rose to his feet. "Are you sure this isn't just an attempt for you to get a great view of my ass?"

Cali jerked the board and Chase flipped into the ocean. He popped out of the water. "What was up with that?"

"I don't know what you're talking about," Cali replied innocently. "You're the one who didn't keep your balance."

Chase jumped up on the board determined not to fall. He faced Cali and slowly started to rise up. "You're doing it backwards."

"I know. I want to keep and eye on you and make sure you don't try anything."

"Like what?"

"Like, trying to flip me off again."

Chase got to his feet. His arms were waving back and forth as he tried to keep his balance. "Just relax a little more."

"Relax? I'm trying not to fall."

"Well, think about something else."

"That's a little hard to do when you're trying not to fall." Cali slowly started to stand up. "What are you doing?" Chase looked at her nervously while he tried to keep his balance.

"Grab my hands."

"What?"

"Grab my hands." Cali held out her hands. "It's something my dad used to do when I first learned how to surf. Look at me."

Chase stared at the water. As much as he'd love to look at her, he didn't want to fall again. "This is some type of trick to tip me over, isn't it?"

Cali grabbed his hands and smiled. "It's not a trick." She could feel his body shaking through his hands as he tried to keep his balance. "You couldn't keep your eyes off me two days ago and now you're refusing to look at me?"

Chase smiled. "I was out of the water at the time." Cali's hands were soft in his. He looked up at her. The water had accented different highlights in her wavy hair and the sun gave it an added golden look.

"Was that so hard?" she smiled.

Chase could feel his body relaxing as he stared at her. "Cali!" Jesse yelled from the shore bringing Chase back to reality. He jerked back and Cali fell into the water on top of him.

Jesse watched Cali pop out of the water. Chase popped up in front of her almost three inches next to her. "Cali!" Jesse yelled again.

Cali smiled and got onto the board. She looked at Jesse standing on the beach with his hands on his hips. "He doesn't look too happy." Chase jumped up on the board.

*****

Cali walked up to Jesse. "Yes?"

Jesse looked at Chase pulling the surfboard out of the water. "The church called to find out if you were coming down today."

"Couldn't I just go down tomorrow?"

"I already told them that you would be down there in an hour."

Chase walked up to them. He could tell that Jesse definitely was not happy. "I should probably get going."

"That would probably be a good thing."

Cali looked at Jesse in amazement. She had never seen him act like this. She picked up her board and followed Chase up to the Surf Shack. She glanced back at Jesse. His eyes were fixed on the two of them. "I'm sorry about Jesse. He usually doesn't act like this."

"It's not that big of a deal. I could tell he didn't like me when I first got here. He kept pulling down the blinds and looking at me." Chase smiled. "I'm sure you usually don't hang out with guys like me."

"No, I don't but Jesse usually does."

"It's not that big of a deal, Cali." Chase opened the door and Cali walked inside. This was it, he was going to change and leave. He might not ever get the chance to see her again. "What are you doing tomorrow?"

"Tomorrow? I don't know." Cali set her board on the counter. "I'm supposed to be painting a room at Jesse's church. Why?"

"Well," she was sweet, innocent and beautiful— there was no way he'd ever get her even close to a bed, "maybe you could teach me some more tomorrow."

"More surfing?" Cali looked at him with surprise. She would hang out with Chase for the rest of her stay if she didn't have other obligations. "Well, I have to start this room at the church. Maybe you could stop by when you're ready to surf and if I'm far enough along than I could stop."

Meeting at a church didn't sound very promising. "I don't know, maybe you could just…"

Cali sighed. "I promise there won't be anyone there to shove God down your throat."

"Where's it at; maybe I'll stop by."

***

Chapter 5

"Where are you going?" Victor looked at Chase's jacket and helmet. Wherever he was going it was going to be a long ride.

"Out."

"Out where?"

"Since when did you start caring about what I'm doing?" Chase shoved his helmet in his backpack.

"Just curious as to where you were all night."

Chase looked his him with confusion. "Grandpa, you're starting to sound like Axel."

"Speaking of Axel, he called last night wondering where you were."

"What'd you tell him?"

"I told him that you're not my kid and you come and go as you please." He stood up and walked over to Chase. "He wanted me to have you call him if I seen you again."

"So did you?"

"No, I'm still trying to figure out where you were if you weren't with Axel." Victor glanced at the backpack. "And why you've been bringing home wet swim trunks the past two nights."

Chase sighed. There was no sneaking around with his grandpa. "I was out with a girl and I'd rather she didn't get involved with Axel or anyone else."

"Sarah?"

Chase shook his head. "Sarah broke up with me on Tuesday."

Victor looked at Chase confused. If he hadn't been hanging out with Sarah then that meant he was hanging out with another girl. And if he was sneaking around to be with this girl that meant that she wouldn't be accepted by the Demons. "You're not going out with a Dragon, are you?"

Chase looked at his with confusion. "Why would you think that?"

"I don't know." The door bell rang. "You've been acting strange the past couple days."

Victor opened then door and sighed. Axel and Ayden were standing on his porch. "We're looking for Chase."

Victor opened the door further and pointed to Chase. Axel walked past him and saw Chase zipping his jacket. "Where are you going?"

Chase looked at Axel. "What do you want?"

"What do I want? I haven't seen you since you for most of the week."

"I've been here."

"Then how come every time I call, you're not?"

Chase shrugged. "I guess you just call at the wrong time."

"Since you're here maybe you can get a bite to eat with me and Ayden?"

"I've already made plans."

"Who did you make plans with? Sarah told us that she hasn't seen you since Tuesday."

"I didn't say that I made plans with anybody."

"Listen, Chase, we know you've got a lot going on right now but…"

"Axel, I'm not interested."

"Are you interested in doing some diving?" Ayden asked.

"Diving?"

Axel sighed and shook his head. "David wants us to dive down to the car tonight and see what we can recover from it."

"You mean his money?" Chase shook his head. "I'm not interested."

Chase walked outside and strapped his backpack onto the back half of his seat. "David doesn't really care if you're interested in retrieving the money. He said you're doing it," Ayden said quickly.

"Tell David that he can get it himself if he wants it so bad."

"It's not a question, Chase; it's a direct order." Ayden lifted his shirt enough to show his gun.

Chase stared at Ayden. He couldn't believe that he was being threatened, especially by Ayden. He

looked at Axel. "Did he seriously just threaten me?"
"Chase, neither one of us wants to do anything to
you so don't make us."
Chase started his motorcycle. "You might as well
get it over with and shoot me here because I'm not
going down to get that money." He took off down the
street. He could see Ayden and Axel getting into their
car.

***

Chase pulled into the church parking lot and
parked his motorcycle by the front door. He walked
inside and down the hallway to the nursery. He
looked in the window on the door. Cali was on the
ground beneath an outline of some animals. He
slowly turned the knob and walked inside. He
walked up to Cali and looked down at her. She was
asleep and she was wearing the same tank top and
overalls that she had been wearing the day before. He
smiled at how peaceful she looked. He bent down
next to her and gently pushed the strands of hair
away from her face.

*What are you doing here, Chase? Just walk away now
and leave her alone.* He sat back and watched her
breathe. *What is wrong with you, Chase? You're
watching a girl sleep and you're content. Axel would
smack you for continuing to hang out with her after not
getting any action.*

Cali stretched and quickly pulled her arms down when she saw Chase. "Chase?" She sat up quickly. "What are you doing here?"

"I thought you might want to get some breakfast but by the looks of it you never had any dinner."

"What time is it?"

Chase looked at his watch. "Almost eight."

Cali yawned. "What are you doing up so early? I thought you never got out of bed before ten."

"Did I say that?" Chase grinned. "I told you, I wanted to take you to get something for breakfast."

Cali looked at the outlines around the room. "I can't. I have to finish the outlines today."

"You can't eat breakfast?"

"I'm not that hungry."

"When was the last time you ate?"

"Um." Cali tried to think of her last meal. "Lunch with you yesterday."

"Lunch? Cali, all you had were some cookies and that was like twenty hours ago."

"I know." She yawned. "I'm just not really hungry."

"What were your plans today?" Chase asked.

Cali sighed and turned to her back. "I have to complete the outlines today."

Chase looked around to him. He could make out some the animals but for the most part it looked like a four-year-old had gone crazy with a pencil. "Do you think you could take a short break?"

Cali smiled. "I already took a break yesterday to go surfing with you."

"And I helped you." Chase objected. "I sharpened your pencils and I watched you draw all day Wednesday."

"And yesterday you whined until I went surfing with you."

Chase lay down next to her. "Would you just have breakfast with me? I promise, I won't whine or ask you to do anything else."

Cali sighed. Chase was a little rough around the edges but it wasn't like he cussed like a sailor. For the most part he was sweet and Cali hadn't found out about anything absolutely horrible in his life. She knew he didn't care too much for his father and his mother had died a couple weeks ago but other than that his life was a mystery. It scared Cali but it also intrigued her. She had never had so much fun with someone or been so happy to see someone more than she was with Chase. She sat up. "All right, I'll get breakfast with you."

"I'm glad you agreed by your own choice because if you hadn't I might have been forced to sway your opinion."

Chase helped Cali to her feet. "And how were you planning on doing that?"

"I don't know, I didn't have to."

Cali pushed him away from her and laughed. "You just think you're God's gift to women now don't you."

Chase laughed. Cali was looked around the room and then looked at Chase blankly. "What's wrong?"

"I forgot that Jesse dropped me off yesterday so I don't have my purse or the jeep."

"Not a problem." Chase held up his motorcycle keys.

Cali stared at the keys. Jesse would kill her if she got of his bike and then her dad would bring her back to life to kill her again. "I don't..."

"I know, you don't think that it's safe," Chase quickly objected. "I brought my helmet and my jacket for you to wear so you won't have to worry about anything."

Cali smiled. Dying couldn't hurt that bad; besides, what would be the point of dying if she hadn't lived a little? She followed Chase out of the church and stared at the motorcycle. It was intimidating. Chase took his helmet out of his backpack and handed it to her. "Do you think I could leave this in the nursery?"

Cali looked at the backpack. "Yeah, I don't know why not."

"Okay, I'll be right back." Chase ran inside.

Cali pulled her hair back into a ponytail and then pulled the helmet on. She strapped it and picked up Chase's coat. Chase walked out and started the motorcycle. He straddled the motorcycle and put the kickstand up. "Go ahead and get on."

Cali stepped up on the peg and sat down behind him. "What do I hold on to?"

"Just hang on to me." Chase smiled and pulled down his sunglasses. Cali put her arms around Chase's chest. He pushed them down to his waist. "I don't want you to pull me off."

Chase felt her take a deep breath. Her arms gripped tighter around his waist as he pulled out of the parking lot.

***

Axel looked at Ayden. "It's the girl that pulled us out of the ocean."

"Do you think she knows anything?"

Axel shook his head. "Chase hasn't told her anything, not with the way he was acting."

Ayden picked up his phone. "Hey, it's Ayden."

"You better have good news," Xavier replied. "David has been all over my case this morning."

Ayden could tell that his father was aggravated. "Chase isn't going to get the money and I think he's trying to skip out on us."

"Skip out on us? Why would Chase want to do that?"

"Sarah said he was talking about going to Mexico."

"Where is he now?"

"He's joyriding through town with some blonde."

"A Demon?"

"No, she's one of the surfers that pulled him and Axel out of the water."

"What the hell is he doing with a surfer?"

"Shit if I know."

"You and Axel get the money back and make sure you keep a close eye on Chase."

Ayden hung up the phone and looked at Axel. "Dad said to get the money ourselves."

Axel watched Chase disappear around a corner. Chase was usually his wingman on every drop and pick up. Not having him along almost seemed like bad luck.

***

"What are you doing?" Chase asked as Cali spread peanut butter across her pancakes.

"I hate pancakes."

"Then why did you want to come to Lenny's House of Pancakes?"

"You said you liked it." Cali licked the peanut butter off the knife. "I'll eat them with peanut butter but they're not on my list of breakfast items."

"Next you're going to tell me that you don't like orange juice." Cali glanced up at him. "No!"

"It's not my first choice. I like grape and apple better."

"Oh, you're killing me." Chase watched her put a piece of peanut butter covered pancakes in her mouth. He shook his head. "You have strange eating habits."

"Me? Aren't you the one who had hot sauce on your French fries?"

"My mom was from Mexico; what do you expect?"

"And your hamburger?"

"I like things spicy; you like things weird. Like a banana and sugar on a piece of bread? How does that constitute as a meal?"

"In Norway that was all I ate for breakfast."

Chase watched her eat her pancakes. She was amazing and nothing like any other girls he had dated. Technically, they weren't dating but she wasn't like any girl he had hung out with. "You never told me how many countries you've actually been to."

"A lot."

"That's not an answer."

Cali wiped some peanut butter off her face and swallowed. "Somewhere around fifty or so. I'd have to write them all down and that would only be the ones I remembered going to."

"Fifty? I don't think I can even name fifty countries. How old are you again?"

"Nineteen."

"Nineteen and you've been to fifty countries? I haven't even made it to all fifty states."

"The only states I've been to...California, Georgia, and Texas. Technically, Georgia and Texas don't count because I've only been to their airports."

"Where were you born?"

"Um, I believe it was Mexico."

"You believe it was Mexico?"

"I don't remember. Mom has told me a bunch of times but it's not on my list of things to remember."

"So, what is your favorite country?"

Cali looked down at her pancakes and tried to think. She had been to so many countries it seemed impossible to choose just one. "I don't think I have a favorite country but Australia has been one of my favorite places to live."

Cali watched Chase eat his pancakes. She still hadn't found anything out about him. There was a reason their lives had crossed paths; she was sure of it. "So, where in Mexico are you planning on going?"

Chase looked up. He hadn't thought about Mexico since he'd gone surfing with Cali. "I'm thinking about postponing the trip."

"Really? Why would you do that?"

Chase shoved a forkful of pancakes into his mouth so he could think of a good answer. He swallowed and looked at Cali. "I've thought about spending some more time with my grandpa. I don't get to see him a lot and I've got some downtime now."

"That's sweet." Chase shrugged. "What is he like?"

"What is he like?"

"Is he one of those grumpy old men that isn't happy about anything or is he one of those old men that are so laid back because they're too old to care?"

Chase laughed. He wasn't sure which to classify his grandpa as. "I think he's a little bit of both."

***

Jesse looked out the window. He watched Cali get off the back of Chase's motorcycle. There was something that didn't settle right about Chase. Cali walked into the nursery followed by Chase. She stopped and Jesse could tell by the look on her face that she wasn't expecting him to be there. "We need to talk?"

Cali looked at Chase. Chase grabbed his backpack. "I'll be outside."

Cali sat down and pulled a pencil from her overalls. "What do you need to talk about?"

"Where have you been?"

"Chase took me out for breakfast."

"Did he stay here last night?"

"What?" Cali looked at Jesse. She couldn't believe what he was suggesting, "Why would Chase stay here?"

"Cali, I don't want him around you anymore."

"Why?"

"I don't know." Jesse shook his head. "There's just something that isn't right about him."

"It's not your choice." Cali focused on her drawing.

"What?"

"It's not your choice." Cali took a deep breath to stay calm. She turned around and looked at Jesse. "It's not your decision who I hang out with."

"Cali, I'm trying to look out for you. There's something about Chase that doesn't sit…"

"It sounds to me like you're trying to accuse me." Cali got up. "If you would rather that I go stay at a hotel I'll go."

"Why would I want you to stay at a hotel?"

"Why do you want to choose who I'm hanging out with?"

"Cali, I don't want anything to happen to you."

"Jesse, what's wrong with hanging out with Chase?"

Jesse looked outside at Chase he was getting onto his motorcycle. "I don't know, Cali. I just don't have a good feeling about him."

"What if he came over and had dinner with us?"

"What?"

"That would give you a chance to get to know him better."

"Cali, I don't want to get to know him. I don't trust him."

"You can't trust him if you don't know him."

"I see the way he looks at you and that's enough for me."

"Jesse, you're not my dad and even if you were I'd still say the same thing. I respect your opinion and I'll be careful around Chase but I'm not going to stop hanging out with him."

"Cali…"

Cali got up and grabbed Jesse's arm. She pulled him to the door. "I'm not going out raising hell." She pushed him out of the nursery. "I'm painting a church and surfing. I need to get back to work so I'm done arguing."

Jesse sighed. "Cali, I'm just trying to look out for you."

"Then look out for me but don't yell at me for having fun." She took a deep breath to hold back tears. "For once in my life I don't have to worry about everybody else. I'm actually doing something that I decided to do and I'm having fun. Why do you have to take that away?" She shut the door and walked over to the wall. She took a deep breath to calm her nerves. Jesse was just trying to help but he was doing it the wrong way. Cali had never done anything spontaneous. She had always done exactly what everyone else expected her to do. It felt good to do something that she wanted to do. She stared at the wall. *God, I don't want to step away from you. I just want to have fun. Why does Jesse have to be so hard on me for having a good time?*

***

Jesse walked outside. *God, I was not planning on dealing with this. Why couldn't you keep her from meeting somebody until she got back home?* Chase was strapping his backpack onto his motorcycle. *And why did it have to be him? Why couldn't you let her meet some good church kid that wouldn't get her into any trouble.* Jesse sighed. Cali wouldn't be happy with some church kid that was a perfect angel; she'd get bored. She had her small moments of rebellion but nothing major ever came up. She was more of an adventurer. She would respect you and listen to every word you had to say but there was no way you could make her be what you wanted her to be. The mold had definitely been broken when she was born, and it had been Cali's choice.

Jesse sighed. He walked over to Chase. Chase put up his kickstand. He glanced at Jesse and shook his head. "Listen, it wasn't Cali's idea to ride..."

Jesse put his hand up. "Do you like spaghetti?"

Chase looked at him with confusion. "What?"

"We're having spaghetti tonight and I know Cali would like it if you joined us."

"I don't know." Chase still couldn't figure Jesse out. He knew that Jesse didn't like him very much and didn't want to get in a fight in front of Cali.

"Listen, I apologize for not being the friendliest person but I would like to set that aside." Jesse could see Cali through the nursery window. "I'm not used to Cali hanging out with guys."

"Cali told me that you're like her second dad so I guess I understand." Chase looked at Cali and then looked at Jesse. "I know that you don't have any reason to trust me but I wouldn't do anything to hurt Cali."

"Right, I'm sure you've said that about all your girlfriends."

Chase shook his head and started his motorcycle. "No, Cali's not my girlfriend. And besides that, she's special."

***

Chase jumped over the couch and dropped down on the leather cushions. He picked up the remote and turned the TV off. "I was watching that."

Chase looked at his grandpa. "I went down to get a new cell phone and my plan had been canceled."

Victor leaned back in his chair. "I had a feeling that would be coming."

"Dad closed all my accounts and canceled all my credit cards."

"You're either in the gang or you're not, Chase."

"Well, what am I supposed to do about money?"

"Go out and get a job."

Chase stared at his grandpa. "You put him up to this didn't you?"

He laughed. "Your dad hasn't talked to me since I turned the Demons over to him."

"He's doing this because I won't go get his stupid money."

"What money?"

"The money from the…" Chase got up and smiled. "Never mind."

"Chase, what money are you talking about?"

Chase grabbed his jacket. "Two can play at this game."

"Chase, whatever you're thinking about doing is not a smart decision especially if it involves David's money."

"It's not David's money if he doesn't have it."

Victor got up. "Chase, think about what you're suggesting. You're going to take David's money and you think he's just going to sit back and watch?"

Chase shrugged. "I can handle myself. It's not like I'm going to flash it around."

Victor grabbed Chase's arm. "You can't take his money."

"I can if he doesn't know about it."

"Chase, he'll find out and when he does…"

"I'm not stupid. I know what I'm doing."

Victor shook his head. Chase had no idea what he was getting himself into. "Son or no son, he'll kill you if he finds out you took his money."

"Then I guess he can't find out."

Victor watched Chase walk out the front door. He dropped down in his recliner. There was no way Chase could get away with this and when he got caught there would be nothing Victor could do to help him.

***

Chase looked at his watch. He was supposed to be at the Surf Shack in an hour. That would give him plenty of time to get the backpack and stash it. He pulled off his jeans and pulled on his wetsuit. He smiled at the red swim trunks. Cali had got to him more than he had realized. He looked at the dark water. Once he got into that water there was no going back to the way things were. Life as he knew it would be gone. *I must be losing my mind. I'm about to throw away everything for a girl.*

Chase waded out in the water and turned on his flashlight. He pulled down the goggles and took a deep breath. The water was cold without the sun to warm it up. He got to the car and swam in the back window. The backpack was sitting on the backseat. He grabbed it and kicked for the surface. His burst out of the water and took in a deep breath. Surfing had helped him learn to hold his breath but that had felt like an eternity. Chase pulled his goggles off and shoved them in his backpack.

Something clicked behind it. It was a sound Chase knew very well. He slowly lifted his hands. "Set the bag down."

Chase turned around. Ayden was standing in front of him with his gun pointed at him. Axel and three other Demons were standing behind him. Two of the Demons circled around and grabbed Chase from behind. "Did you guys come down for a swim too?"

One of the guys kicked him in his side. Ayden stared at Chase. He walked up to him. "Did you get this to buy your new girlfriend some presents?"

"Don't even..." Ayden pushed his gun into Chase's forehead.

"Give me the backpack."

Axel stepped closer. "Just hand the backpack to Ayden, Chase. We'll take you back to the house and tell David that it was all a misunderstanding."

Chase looked at Axel. If he went back he would be stuck again and he wouldn't be able to live with that. Cali had opened a door for him to get away from the Demons. Chase spit in Ayden's face and then grabbed his wrist and spit on Ayden's gang tattoo.

Ayden wiped the spit off his face and stared at Chase. He looked at the two guys holding Chase and then looked at Chase. They pushed Chase down in the sand and one of the guys kicked him in the side. One of the guys grabbed his hair and shoved his face into the sand.

Chase gasped as his face was pulled out of the sand. He coughed up sand and wiped his eyes to get it out. One of the guys punched him in the face and another kicked him in the side. "Tomorrow you're going to come back to the house," he could hear Ayden say between the jabs and kicks. "You're going to tell David that you were drunk and you weren't in your right state of mind."

"Like hell I will," Chase managed to get out through the pain.

Ayden kicked Chase back and the two guys shoved him against the pier. The third guy punched Chase in the stomach. Ayden walked up to him. "You'll do it or next we'll visit your girlfriend."

Chase pulled at the guys holding him with all the strength he had left. "Leave Cali out of this; she doesn't have anything to do with it."

"She probably doesn't even know what you dragged her into does she?"

"I swear if you lay one finger on her…" One of the guys punched Chase in the face.

"I don't think you're in a position to be making threats." Ayden leaned in close to Chase's face, "I have a feeling that if your little 'good girl' finds out who you really are she'll make an excuse not to see you anymore. So if I was you I'd show my face back at the house."

***

Cali crawled into her hammock. She had spent all day drawing at the church and now her arms felt like modeling clay. Jesse walked by the room and then looked in. "Do you want me to shut this light out?"

"Yes, please." She yawned and pulled the covers up. "I thought you said Chase was coming over tonight."

"I thought that he was." Jesse shut the light off. "Maybe something came up."

Cali yawned again. "Maybe."

"Good night." Jesse pulled the door shut.

Cali closed her eyes and tried to relax. Her body was so tired it'd be hard to get to sleep. She opened her eyes and stared at the ceiling feeling like something was wrong. *God, be with Mom and Dad. Protect them and keep them safe,* she prayed. An image of Chase popped into her head. "Watch out for Chase and be with him. Show me how I can help him."

Cali heard the doorbell ring. "Cali!"

Cali jumped out of bed and ran into the living room. "Jesse, what's…" Jesse was helping Chase to the couch. Chase's wetsuit was torn and dripping with blood. Cali ran up to him. "What happened?"

"Cali, go get some towels and a blanket from the closet."

"But…"

"Now!" Jesse yelled. "And a bottle of water."

Cali ran into the bathroom and grabbed a stack of beach towels and a blanket. She set them on the couch and ran into the kitchen for a bottle of water. She ran back out and looked at Jesse. "Spread the blanket across the couch."

Cali spread the blanket across the couch and Jesse laid Chase down on the couch. Chase's face looked like it had been smashed into a wall. One of his eyes was completely swollen shut and lip was split open. Jesse poured some water of the end of one towel and dabbed the blood off his face.

Chase tried to say something but coughed out blood instead. Cali knelt down next to him and grabbed his hand. "Don't talk. Jesse will fix you up and you'll be okay."

Chase tried to concentrate on Cali's hand in his as Jesse dabbed his face. His whole body was pulsating with pain. It even hurt to breathe. "This might sting a little," he heard Jesse say. He felt something drip on his cheek and then his face burned like it was on fire. He jerked to get away from the pain but that only magnified its intensity.

Jesse ran his hands down Chase's sides. Chase jerked back and forth to get out of his grip. "Try to stay still. I need to see if you broke any bones." Nothing shifted when he ran his hands on his sides and Chase didn't scream about him touching him. "I don't think you broke anything but you'll probably have to get an x-ray to know for sure."

Chase looked at Cali's face. Her bright blue eyes were glassed over with tears. One slipped from her eye and she brushed it away.

"You should drink some water to get the blood out of your mouth." Jesse handed him a bottle of water. "I need to know if it's from inside your mouth or if you're coughing it up."

Chase reached out for the bottle but couldn't get it in focus. Cali grabbed it and put it to his mouth. The water wasn't that cold but it felt cool running into his mouth. He took a couple sips and then dropped his head back on the pillow.

Jesse put his hand on Cali's shoulder. "He should rest."

Cali nodded without looking away from Chase. His eyes were closed but his face still revealed the pain he was in. "I think I'll just sit out her for a little while."

Jesse nodded and walked to the hall. He looked at Cali. Her head was resting on the couch next to Chase's arm. He walked down the hall and shut his door.

***

Chapter 6

Chase tried to open his eyes. They felt like they were weighed down with lead. His right eye finally opened but his left eye refused. He touched his eye and felt the swelling. He looked down at his other arm and saw blonde hair draped over it. He turned his head so he could get a better look with his right eye. Cali's had her arms wrapped around Chase's left arm. Her chest was sitting on his arm and her head was leaning against his side. With her blonde hair and smooth skin, she looked like an angel sitting next to him.

Cali felt Chase's arm move and realized she had fallen asleep. She opened her eyes and sat up. Chase was looking at her through one eye and his other eye was swollen shut. "Are you okay?"

Chase nodded. He felt like someone had run over him and then backed up to do it again. "I'm sorry for coming here. I..."

Cali shook her head. "No, Chase, it's fine. What happened to you?"

Chase thought back to the pier and sat up. "I should probably leave."

"You're not going anywhere looking like this; you need to rest. You look worse than when you flew off the pier."

Every moment he stayed with her was a moment she would be in danger. He stood up. Cali grabbed his arm. Her fingers felt like needles pressing into his arm. He grabbed her hand and pulled it away from his arm. "I have to go."

"Chase, don't go." Cali followed him to the door. Chase reached for the door knob and she put her hand on the door. "Please, let me help you."

Chase sighed. He looked into Cali's eyes. They weren't bright and shiny as usual. They were filled with hurt. Chase opened the door and stumbled outside. *She really cares about me.* Cali walked out next to him. "Please don't leave. Just stay here; you don't have to tell me what happened."

Chase grabbed Cali's hands. "I need to leave." Chase let go of her hands and stepped forward to walk away. Cali wrapped her arms around him and laid her head against his chest. Once she realized what she was doing she couldn't stop. Chase stood with his arms out in bewilderment. *Don't let her pull you in, Chase. You've got to be cold; you have to for her.* He gently grabbed Cali's arms and pulled her back. Tears were sliding down her cheeks. Chase took a deep breath to keep from wrapping her in his arms. Every tear that slid down her cheek felt like a hook latching on to his heart. *You can't bring her into this.*

"Please don't leave." Cali could feel her throat tighten as she tried to hold back from bawling. "I don't want you to leave. If you leave now, you won't come back."

"Why do you think that?"

"I just know."

"Cali, come on." *Be hard, Chase, keep it together.* "Let's just be honest with each other. This wasn't going anywhere. You'll be leaving and then I'll still be here."

Cali looked up at the sky and brushed away her tears. *Why are you so upset? Chase is right, you'll be leaving in two weeks anyway.*

Do you really believe that?

Cali looked at Chase. She had fallen for him. It had only been a week but she had fallen head over heels acting like a fool in love. She shook her head. *God, this is not what was supposed to happen.*

Why?

I wasn't supposed to fall for him. I was supposed to help him.

Do you think that is not helping him?

Cali stared at Chase. The first couple hours they had spent together he was completely distant. She didn't know a lot about his life or background but she knew that she loved him and whatever luggage he carried with him. "I won't leave; I'll stay."

Chase looked at her with confusion. "Cali?"

"I love you, Chase. I can't explain how or why I just know I do and I know that you love me." Cali grabbed his hand. "Tell me that you don't love me."

Chase shook his head. She was right but that wasn't something he could admit. "No, we can't love each other. We're from completely different worlds."

"Chase…"

Chase pulled away. "I have to go." He walked toward the pier without looking back. His heart felt like it had been tossed in a blender. *She's just like any other girl, Chase. Just let her go and move on.*

***

Cali walked into the Surf Shack. Tears slid down her cheeks but she was too upset to care. She walked into her room and lay down on the hammock. She pulled the covers up to her chin and pushed her foot against the wall to rock herself. It wasn't supposed to happen like this. She wasn't supposed to fall in love with him.

Jesse knocked on the door frame. "Are you all right?"

Cali stared at the wall. There was nothing she could do to change anything that had happened. "You were right. I never should have got involved with Chase."

"Cali, maybe you should…"

"I'm going down to the church." She got up and pulled a sweatshirt on over her tank top. "Will you give me a ride?"

"Cali, you don't have to go down there. You can take a break."

"No! I need to go down there." Cali wiped the tears out of her eyes. "I just don't want to think about it. I was stupid. I let myself fall into it."

***

Chase walked up the front steps and opened the front door. He felt like he had been filled to the point of busting and then sucked dry to the bone. His whole body felt numb and it wasn't from the bruising. He walked inside and went to the kitchen. Axel and one of the guy's that held Chase back were sitting at the table eating breakfast.

"Well, look what the cat drug in."

Chase stared at Matt. He hadn't been with the Demons very long but Chase knew that he had a problem with keeping his mouth shut. Chase walked up to the cupboard next to the fridge and grabbed a gun out of it. He tucked it in to the back of his pants and walked out of the kitchen. Axel walked out after him. "Chase?" He grabbed his arm. "Chase…"

Chase swung around and punched him in the face. "Don't ever touch me again or I'll kill you."

"Don't you think you're overreacting?" Axel grabbed the coffee table to pull himself up. Chase kicked him in the side and he dropped back to the ground. A gun clicked above him. Axel looked up and saw Matt standing in the kitchen doorway with his gun aimed at Chase.

Chase spread his arms. "Do it!"

"Put you gun away, Matt." Axel jumped up. He grabbed Chase's arm and pushed him down on couch before he could fight back. "Cool off!"

"He shouldn't even be here. Ayden should have taken him out under the pier but he didn't have the..."

"You shut your mouth!"

"He doesn't deserve to be a Black Demon."

Chase jumped up and Axel held him back. "Why don't you throw down your gun and say that to my face?"

"The only reason you're still here is because your dad is the leader. If it had been anyone else Ayden would have taken them out no questions asked," Matt yelled. "All you do is sit around and get lap dances while the rest of us bust our asses to make money for your dad. We give up everything while you sit there."

"Matt, shut up!"

Chase tried to reach past Axel. His fingers came inches from Matt's face. Axel pushed him back. "Chase!"

"What is going on?" Ayden yelled.

Chase pushed Axel off him and backed up. "How long have you been with the Demons?"

"What?"

Chase paced back and forth in front of Axel. He stared at Matt. "How long have you been with the Demons?"

"Almost two years."

"Two years? Two years and you think you bust your ass?" Chase ducked past Axel and grabbed Matt by the front of his shirt. Axel pulled Chase away from him. "I was born a Demon. Don't tell me that I don't bust my ass. I've given up everything for them."

"You mean that little blonde bitch?"

Chase lunged at Matt. Ayden and Axel pushed him back into the wall. "Matt, get out of here now!"

Matt rolled his eyes and walked out of the house slamming the front door. Ayden and Axel let go of Chase. He pushed past them, walked up to his bedroom and slammed his door. He looked at his room. A picture of him and his mom was sitting on the dresser. He had taken it from his mom's things that were being thrown out. His dad had thrown away all her things in an attempt to move on. Chase sunk to the ground.

He thought about Cali's smile and tears swelled up in his eyes. He took a deep breath and brushed them away. *Stop being such a pansy, Chase; you barely even knew her. If Cali knew what you really were she wouldn't want anything to do with you.* He did love her and there was no way he could be with her without putting her in danger.

He looked up and saw himself in the mirrors on his closet doors. She was sweet and innocent. He was a Demon. He always had been and he always would be. He had dreamed of leaving and his dreams had been beat out of him. The Demons had taken everything from him—his mother, his love, and his life. He hated them. He pulled the gun from the back of his pants and threw it at the mirrors.

***

Chapter 7

Jesse walked into the nursery. Cali was brushing furiously at the wall. She had one whole wall complete. She looked at him and then went back to painting. Her eyes were droopy from lack of sleep. Her skin was pale and splattered with paint. "Why don't we go get some lunch?"

"I'm good."

"Cali, you can't stay down here all day, you need to take a break."

"I'm fine." She yawned. "I have to get this done."

"Cali, you've been down here since yesterday morning. I know you're upset but you can't do this to yourself."

"I don't want to talk about it." Cali sighed.

"Will you at least take a break?"

Cali looked at the paintbrushes in her overalls. She was tired and she was wearing herself out. She was trying so hard to get over the hurt that she was actually hurting herself. "Something to eat sounds good."

***

Chase sat down across from Axel. "Listen, Chase, I'm sorry about what happened."

Chase looked at Axel. No matter how much he wanted to be upset with him he couldn't. "If you tried to help they would have killed us both."

"Ayden would never have shot you."

"Let's not talk about it." Chase looked around the restaurant. An older couple sat down at a booth across the room. Chase looked at Axel to get his mind off of the couple. "What are we doing today?"

"We have three small drops." Axel's cell phone rang. "Hello?" Chase looked out the window. Axel held out the cell phone to him. He looked at him with confusion. "It's for you." He shrugged.

"Hello?"

"Is this, the Chase Laney?" a man with an Asian accent asked.

"Who wants to know?"

"I have a business proposition for you."

"Who is this?"

"I heard that you were the man to go to if you needed money."

Chase laughed. "I don't know who you heard that from."

"Are you David Laney's son?"

Chase rolled his eyes in annoyance. "When I have to be. Now who is this?"

"I want you to meet me at Mama Fu's Restaurant downtown in one hour. I suggest you stop at the bank first and because you'll need to make a withdrawal."

Chase laughed. "All right, cut the shit, who is this?"

"I work for Chang Li."

Chase laughed. Chang was one of the Red Dragons' leaders, a rival gang that worked out of the downtown area but had originated from China. "How much money are you hitting me up for and why?" Chase decided to plan along.

"Five hundred thousand dollars. It's a small fee for trespassing on Dragon territory."

"Trespassing? We had an exchange and your boys double-crossed us."

"I was referring to your surfing lessons."

***

Cali hopped out of the jeep. "Are you sure you don't want to go surfing? It will get your mind off things."

"Jesse, I'm fine. Painting will help me keep busy and once I get done I'll be able to relax."

"I'll be back at five to pick you up."

"Okay." Cali shut the door. "Can we have burgers?"

"I guess so. Are you sure you don't want me to stick around with you?"

"Jesse, you will get so bored you'll drive me crazy. I'll be fine."

"Okay." Jesse sighed and pulled out of the parking lot.

Cali walked into the church and down the dark hallway. She opened the door to the nursery and turned on the light. She walked up to the wall and lay down to take in the whole picture. *God, I'm never going to finish this in time.* An image of Chase popped into her head. She quickly stood up and grabbed her paintbrushes. She had to stay busy to keep from thinking about Chase. She picked up her brush and looked at the elephant on the wall.

"It looks like it's coming along pretty good." Cali turned around and saw the woman in charge of the nursery.

"I think I'm going to start on the ark tomorrow."

"This is so great, Cali. I love it."

"Hopefully, I'll have it done before next Sunday so you can have the room back."

She smiled. "There's no hurry, you've already got so much done." She walked out of the nursery and Cali turned back to the wall.

Cali heard the door open again. "I was thinking about putting a giraffe..." Someone covered her mouth. She reached for the hand and tried to pull it away. Something covered her eyes and mouth. Her hands were pulled behind her back and she felt something wrap around them.

***

"Chase, what is going on?" Axel yelled as Chase cut through traffic. Chase turned the corner and saw Surf Shack with flames escaping through the windows. He pulled into the drive and ran up to the house. "Cali?"

Chase ran around the house and looked in every window that the fire allowed him to. It didn't seem like anybody was inside. He looked at the parking lot. Jesse's jeep was gone. *The church.* Chase jumped back in the car and sped out of the parking lot.

"Chase, where are you going?"

"I don't think they have her yet."

"What are you talking about?"

"One of Chang's boys called me on your phone. He wants five hundred thousand dollars."

"Wait, Chase, why would they call my phone to get you?"

"I don't have a phone."

"How would they know that?"

Chase looked at the flashing lights ahead of him and he felt his heart drop. He swerved to the side of the road and jumped out of the car. "Chase!" Axel jumped out of the car and grabbed Chase. "What are you doing; there's cops all over the place."

Chase shook him off and ran up to the accident. An officer stopped him before he reached the jeep. "I'm sorry you can't go any farther."

Chase looked past the officer. Jesse's jeep was

sitting between two ambulances. "Did anybody get hurt?"

"I'm not sure."

"Where's there anybody in the jeep?"

The officer looked at Chase. "I'm not sure."

"I'm looking for a girl. She has blonde hair."

The officer shook his head. "I just got here."

Chase looked at the accident. A stretcher was being loaded into an ambulance. Chase ran past the officer and ran up to the stretcher. Jesse's head was covered in blood and his eyes were darting from left to right. "Jesse?"

"Who...who's there?"

"What's wrong with him?" Chase asked the EMT.

"We believe he's experiencing loss of vision but we haven't determined the cause yet."

Chase looked at Jesse. "Jesse, where's Cali? Was she with you?"

"No, she's at the church. I dropped off at the church."

"Sir, you're going to have to come with me." The officer grabbed Chase's arm.

Chase felt someone grabbed his hand. He looked down at Jesse. "Chase?"

"Yeah?"

"If anything happens to me, promise me you'll look out for Cali until she leaves."

"Jesse, you're going to be..."

"Promise me."

"I'll pick her up right now and we'll both come up to the hospital."

Jesse nodded slowly and the EMTs pushed the stretcher into the ambulance. The officer pulled Chase back to the crime scene barricades and pushed him on the other side. "Do not pass these barricades again."

Axel grabbed Chase's arm and pulled him away from the tape. He held out his cell phone. Chase grabbed the cell phone. "You hung up on me. Not a very smart thing to do for a man in your position."

"Why are you doing this?" Chase walked back to the car.

"For the money; why else would we be doing this?"

"If you want the money then I'll get you the money just leave her out of this."

"Ah, then my sources were right and you do care about this girl."

"I swear to God if you lay one finger on her I will…"

"You're not in a position to be making threats. I want you to get the money and meet me at Mama Fu's. You have forty-five minutes."

"Even if I did have that kind of money I couldn't get it in forty-five minutes." The phone line went dead. Chase threw the phone down and it shattered against the sidewalk.

"Chase?"

Chase sunk down into the driver's seat and stared out the window. There was no way his dad would give him that kind of money. He had pulled Cali into a war he couldn't win and she was going to be the one who paid for it.

***

Chapter 8

Cali felt someone touch her arm and she jerked to get away. "Do you think you can keep your mouth shut if I take the tape off?"

Cali nodded and the tape was ripped from her mouth. She winced with pain and tried to move away. She couldn't hear anyone else in the room except whoever had taken the tape off her mouth. "Why are you doing this?"

"I told you to keep quiet," the man said with a hint of an Asian accent in his voice.

Cali looked in the direction of the voice. "Are you from China?"

"Why would you ask that?" Another voice asked.

"I think you've made a mistake. I don't know who you think I am."

She could hear the voice snicker. "And who are you?"

"I'm the daughter of Troy and Lily Sterling. They're missionaries."

"And why should this concern me, Miss Sterling?"

Cali tried to look in the direction of the voice. "Well, if you're looking to collect a ransom..."

"People kidnap girls for other things."

Cali was aware of the reasons people kidnapped girls. She had been in countries were they were taken and raped or sold into prostitution. *God, please take care of me. Speak to these men and let them have a change of heart.* Cali heard the men talking in Mandarin. She tried to think of the few words that she knew from her trip to China. "God loves you more than you can know," she said in Mandarin.

The tape across her eyes got ripped off and she screamed. She blinked until everything came into focus. "Where did you learn to say that?"

Cali looked at the men. Their spiky, coal-black hair, slanted eyes, and facial features made them almost identical. She was trying to mentally memorize their faces. "I learned in China."

A door opened behind her. Cali turned her head to look at who had come in and one of the guys turned her face forward and put the tape back on her eyes. "What are you doing?"

"She speaks Mandarin."

"You can't let her see you." The other voice was American. Cali heard duct tape being tore off the roll. Something pressed against her eyes and hair. She heard the two guys talking back and forth in

Mandarin again. "Hey, what'd I tell you about speaking that shit in front of me?"

"Why are you doing this?" Cali tried to stay calm.

"We're just trying to make a living, the easy way."

"I just told them I don't have any money."

She felt a hand run up the inside of her leg. She tried to pull away but her legs were taped to the chair legs. "Don't touch me!" Cali screamed.

Something hard slapped her face. "You need to learn to shut that pretty mouth of yours." She felt a hand clamp around her chin. "We could have a little fun if you lightened up."

"God loves you," Cali said in Mandarin.

"What did she say?"

"God loves you." Cali repeated. *Please, God, speak to their hearts.*

Something hard slapped her face again. "Enough!" She heard the two guys speaking in Mandarin again. Something in the room clicked. "What did she say?"

"'God loves you,'" one of the men translated. "We should go see Chang to find out about the money."

"You go do that; I'll watch her." Cali heard the door shut. "God loves you? They kidnapped you and that's what you tell them?"

"God loves you, too!"

"If God loves you so much then why are you here? In case you haven't noticed this isn't a five star hotel." He ran his hand up her thigh and then unsnapped her overalls. She felt his lips touch her neck and she jerked away.

"You don't want to do this."

She heard duct tape being ripped off a roll. "There are a lot of things that I don't want to do, but this is definitely not one of them." The tape got pressed against her mouth. Cali tried to scream through the tape. He pulled down her overalls. "You should look at this as a gift from God. I'm doing you a favor."

Cali pulled at the tape behind her back. She could feel the tears gathering between her eyes and the duct tape. *Please, God, make it stop! Please!* She felt his hands slid up her bare legs and then up her shirt. The door in the room opened and the hands left her shirt. "What the hell?"

"Chang wants to see the girl."

"Well, tell Chang that I'm not done with her and he doesn't have any business with her in the first place." She felt his hands go up her shirt to the back of her bra. "Do you mind finding somewhere else to go?"

Please don't let him leave. Cali cried.

She heard the door shut and she felt her bra pop loose. *Please, God, don't let this happen.* He grabbed her panties and the door opened again. Someone walked into the room and she heard a loud thud. "If you want to be with a woman than go pick one up on the street and pay for it." Cali felt the tape being gently pulled off her mouth. "Do you speak Mandarin?" the man asked her in perfect English. Cali nodded. "Where are you from?"

"My parents are missionaries. I've been to China a lot but I don't live there."

"Who taught you to speak Mandarin?" She felt something lie across her exposed skin.

"We went to a village just outside of Handan. There was an older woman in the village who couldn't speak any English so I asked the children how to say some things so I could talk to her."

"Handan? When did you go to this village?"

It was hard to think after everything that had happened. "I...I don't remember...maybe...five years ago."

"Really?" Cali couldn't see the man but he sounded intrigued.

Cali tried to think back to the trip. She had taken so many since then. "We stayed at the village for a week and talked to people about God. The older lady, the one who couldn't speak English, she gave her life to God and a lot of other people did too."

"What was her name?"

Cali thought back to the village. "Um...Ming. Chang Ming, you know because the names reversed over there."

"This woman, did she have a scar on her left check?" Cali looked at him with confusion and nodded. He stepped back and looked at someone behind her. He yelled something in Mandarin and then pulled out a knife. "Five years ago, a man and a woman pulled up to a village outside of Handan. The man helped the men of the village fix up their houses and the woman helped the women of the village cook meals." Cali looked at the knife nervously. "They brought a girl with them and she played with the children in the village."

He walked behind her. "That same girl would go into the house of an elderly lady and bring her flowers every day. She would tell the woman, 'God loves you, more than you can know.'" Cali felt the tape being cut off her hands. She reached for the tape on her eyes and someone grabbed her hands. "I can't let you do that if you want to leave."

Cali felt the tape around her ankles being taken off. "That woman was my grandmother."

***

Chase walked into the warehouse. The caller had changed the location at the last minute and told Chase to meet him at an abandoned warehouse that the Dragons and Demons did most of their drug exchanges at. There was a light on in the back of the warehouse and three men were standing by the wall. "I don't like the looks of this, Chase."

"Axel, I don't have any other choice."

Axel set his hand on his gun and followed Chase towards the men. One of the men pointed a gun at Chase. "Kick your weapons over to us and lie down on the ground."

Chase pulled his gun out of the back of his pants. "What are you doing, Chase?"

"Axel, do what they ask."

Axel looked at the men. "How do you know it's not a set-up?" Axel whispered. "How do we know you actually have the girl?"

They heard a car door open and Chang Li walked into the light. "Hold your weapons where I can see them."

"Where's Cali, Chang?"

He looked at them and shook her head. "I did not do anything to her. Some of my men were involved in her kidnapping and for that they will be dealt with."

Axel looked at Chase with confusion. "Where's she at, Chang?"

"She's safe. However…"

Chase pointed the gun at him. "Where is she at, Chang?"

"She's safe." Chang repeated. "However, I need to speak with you in private. No guns, no bodyguards."

"You're not going anywhere." Axel shook his head.

Chase handed his gun to Axel and walked up to Chang. Chang motioned him to a seat at the table and waved his men away. Chase sat down at the table. "Where did you find this girl?"

Chase looked at him with confusion. "Listen, just cut the shit. I came here to get Cali back."

"Then answer the question."

"Some of your boys rammed us off the pier and she pulled us out of the water. You have to let her go. She doesn't have anything to do with the Demons. I couldn't get you the money but you can do whatever you want to me. I just need you to let her go."

"Need me to let her go?" Chang laughed. "Of all the deals and peace swaps I've done with your family I have never once heard you talk like this."

"I got her into this. She doesn't know anything about the Demons and she's of no use to you so just let her go. You can take me in her place."

"So it's true, then?" Chang sat back in his chair. "You do have a thing for this girl?"

"I just want you to let her go, untouched."

Chang sighed. "I'm afraid there's going to be a problem with that. There was a guy working with my boys that tried to…"

Chase jumped up. "I swear I will kill whoever…"

"Sit down, Chase! It wasn't one of my boys. It was an outside guy. I got her out of the room before anything happened." Chase sat down. "I have my reasons for doing what I am about to do and I don't want them to be questioned. Your father and I have had an understanding and do our best to keep the peace between the Dragons and Demons. The girl trusts you and I'm turning her over to you to take her out of here. I want her to remain blindfolded until you're out of the downtown area." Chang stood up.

Chase stood up in amazement. Chang walked into the darkness and returned with Cali. She had duct tape wrapped around her eyes and hair. Chase ran up to her and wrapped his arms around her. "Are you okay?"

"Chase?" Cali reached for the duct tape.

"You have to leave it on for now. Come on." Chase looked at Chang and then turned to Axel. He grabbed Cali's hand and walked her out of the warehouse. He handed the keys to Axel and got in the back seat with Cali. Cali leaned against his chest. Chase could hear her crying softly. He wrapped his arms around her and tried to hold back the tears. It was his fault she was crying. He had brought her into this. "Axel, stop at Grandpa's."

***

Chase gently pulled the duct tape off her eyes. Cali pressed her head against his chest and wrapped her arms around him. Chase pulled her back. "Cali, I can't do this. I'm the reason they took you."

Cali nodded. "You're in a gang."

"Chang told you?"

"He asked me how I met you and asked if I knew what you were. He told me that you're in a gang; your dad is the leader."

Chase looked at the ground. "Yes."

Cali knelt down in front of him and looked up at him. "Chase, I still love you."

"You can't." Chase sat back. How could she still love him? She had almost been raped and it had been his fault. "You can't love me."

Cali took his face in her hands and forced him to look at her. "I love you." She felt the tears swelling up in her eyes. "I don't know this gang person; I know you and that's who I love."

Chase stood up and pushed her aside. "That's who I am, Cali. I'm a Black Demon. Just like my dad is, and my grandfather and great-grandfather were. I can't change that," Chase yelled. He looked at Cali. The tears running down her cheeks were building tears up in his eyes. "I've done horrible things. Things that I don't want anyone to know about, especially you. You don't deserve to be with me. You deserve to be with some pastor who's grown up in church his whole life and never done anything wrong."

"No!" Cali cried and wrapped her arms around Chase. "I want to be with you."

"You can't!" Chase let the tears go. "You can't! I'm a horrible person and you don't deserve me."

Cali grabbed his face and looked into his eyes. "You are whoever you choose to be. Tonight, you were willing to trade spots with me and in my book that makes you anything but a horrible person."

"Cali…"

Cali put her hand to his mouth. "Don't tell me that you can't be with me because you're a horrible person. You're not."

"Because of me Jesse is in the hospital and the Surf Shack has been reduced to ashes."

Matt walked into the room with his gun pointed at Chase. Axel stood up in confusion. "Matt, what are you doing here?"

Matt fired the gun and Axel dropped back in the chair. Blood was dripping from his right arm. Chase looked at Axel, glad that Matt was horrible with guns. He looked at Matt who was now dripping sweat and swaying nervously. "Matt, what are you doing?"

"I liked your idea, Chase." Matt wiped his forehead. "I was getting sick of the Demons. Running away to Mexico sounded like a plan but unlike you, I don't have the kind of cash that you have."

Cali gasped. That voice, she recognized that voice. She grabbed Chase's arm and stepped behind him. Chase glanced at her with confusion. "Cali?"

"It's him, Chase. He's the one that tried to rape me."

Chase looked at in disbelief. "You?"

"That's right. I was the one that planned her kidnapping. I got with Chang and told him that I'd give him half the money if he gave me two guys to help kidnap her."

"And you tried to rape her?" Chase reached forward but Cali pulled him back.

Matt held the gun up at Chase. His arm was shaking furiously. "That's right!" Matt wiped the sweat off his forehead. "You could do anything you wanted and nobody would so much as look at you while the rest of us had to devote everything to the Demons. I wanted to make you suffer the way of the rest of us had to."

Cali saw Victor step into the hallway behind Matt. He saw the gun and pulled Matt's arm toward the ceiling. Matt dropped the gun and Victor held him in a headlock. Chase picked up the gun and pointed it at Matt. Cali grabbed his arm. "Chase, no!"

Matt tried to pull away from Victor but Victor tightened his grip. Matt began to throw punches in the air as if he were fighting an invisible opponent. "Chase, he's stoned out of his mind," Victor objected. "There's no point in killing him."

"No point in killing him? What about what he put Cali through?"

Cali grabbed Chase's arm. "Chase, don't." Chase looked at the tears rolling down her cheeks. There was no way he could let Matt live knowing what he tried to do to her. "Please," Cali pulled at his arm, "I want to leave. I want to go see Jesse now."

"We'll go see Jesse." Cali stepped in front of him. Chase lowered the gun. "Cali, get out of the way."

"If you kill him then you're no better than he is."

"No better than him? Cali, he tried to rape you."

"And you're going to kill him, Chase." Cali put her hand on his. "Take him to the police and let them handle it."

"So he can get a slap on the wrist? They're not going to take care of him, Cali. Not the way he should be taken care of."

"However they take care of him will be better than his blood being on your hands."

Chase lowered the gun. As much as he wanted to kill Matt he couldn't do it in front of Cali. Cali wrapped her arms around him. He watched his grandpa drag Matt out of the room.

***

Axel looked at the bandage wrapped around his arm. "I can't believe it went straight through my tribal band."

"At least it didn't go straight through your heart."

The door opened and Cali walked in. Chase stood up. "How is Jesse doing?"

"His sight is back to normal now. The doctor thinks that he had a pinched nerve." Cali sighed. "He's pretty banged up but I think he'll be okay."

Cali walked up to Chase and wrapped her arms around him. She was trying her hardest to hold everything together and what she needed more than anything was just to know that someone else was there for her.

Chase looked at Axel. He stared at the gang tattoo on Axel's wrist and then looked down at his own. The tattoo was a cruel reminder of what he had to do. He grabbed Cali's arms and stepped back from her. "Cali, we still can't be together."

"Chase?"

"It's my fault. I never should have got involved with you in…"

"No." Cali shook her head. "Don't even say that."

"Cali, you're going back to Australia in a week."

"I'll stay."

Chase stared at Cali in disbelief. "Cali, your family's in Australia."

"They'll understand." Cali grabbed Chase's hands like she had on the surfboard. "I love you, Chase. The only way I'm leaving is if you tell me that you don't love me back."

***

Chapter 9

Chase stared at the TV. The channels were flipping so fast that he only caught a second of each show. "What are you doing?"

"Watching TV," Chase replied without looking up.

Axel took the remote from him. "Doesn't watching it require you to stop on a station?"

"He's been watching it like that every day," his grandpa yelled from the kitchen. "I'm ready to have the cable disconnected."

Axel looked at Chase. He was wrapped up in a blanket on the couch. "Have you eaten anything?"

"Yes."

"Really? What did you eat?"

"I had a bowl of cereal."

"That was yesterday." His grandpa walked into the room and sat down in his recliner. "He refuses to eat and refuses to leave that couch."

"Why not just use a gun; it's faster."

Chase stared at the blank TV screen. "Using a gun would be painless."

"Chase, look at yourself. You look horrible. I bet you haven't shaved at all this week have you?"

"Just leave me alone, Axel."

"I brought something that might cheer you up." Axel tossed a newspaper on the coffee table.

"At this point, nothing can cheer me up."

Axel opened the newspaper and held it in front of Chase's face. Matt's picture was in the newspaper. "Why is this supposed to make be happy?"

"He got life in prison."

"He'll get out on parole."

"I doubt he'll last long enough to get out. The cell block that they put him on is packed with Red Dragons."

Chase sighed. The satisfaction of Matt getting the crap beat out of him every day was overshadowed by the though of never seeing Cali again.

"Isn't Cali supposed to be leaving today?"

Chase rolled over and faced the back of the couch. "I don't want to talk about it."

"Why don't you just talk to her?"

Chase sat up. "You saw what happened. I couldn't live with myself if something happened to her again."

"Then get on with your life."

"What?"

"You heard what I said. Get on with your life. Are you just going to lie on your grandpa's couch until you die?"

"Please don't give him any ideas."

"Chase, you need to get on with your life whatever you decide to do."

"How do you expect me to just get on with my life?" Chase jumped up. "What life? My mom's dead, my dad might as well be because I never talk to him, and I don't even know who I am."

"Your mom's death wasn't your fault, Chase," Axel objected. "The store got robbed; if you had been there then you would probably be dead too."

"I might as well be."

"Don't say that."

Chase rolled over and looked at Axel. "Well, I should be. I lied to the only girl who ever loved me not because I was a Demon but because I was me."

"You still have a chance to be somebody." His grandpa looked at Axel.

Axel pulled an envelope out of his pocket and handed it to Chase. Chase opened the envelope and then looked at them. "What's this?"

"It's your chance to be who you want to be."

"I can't."

"Why can't you?" Axel yelled. "This is what you want. I know it; he knows it. You're the only one who won't admit it, Chase."

***

Cali pulled her bag from the trunk and looked at Jesse. He was wiping his eyes. "Don't start."

"Start what? I got glue in my eye," Jesse objected.

Cali looked at the gash next to Jesse's eye. It looked gruesome. Stitches to keep it together and then glue on top of that. "Jesse, you're not allowed to start crying until I get on the plane and can't see you anymore. You know if you start that you're just going to make me start."

Jesse pulled the ticket out of his pocket. "I'm not crying. I'm watering my cheeks."

Cali laughed and tears swelled up in her eyes. She blinked them away. "Come on, you're going to make me late for checking in."

Cali walked into the airport and walked up to the check-in counter. Jesse's phone rang. "Hello?"

Cali handed her tickets to the clerk. "Australia? That will be a nice vacation."

"Oh, I live in Australia."

She smiled and handed her the tickets back. "Well, you have a nice flight home."

Cali turned and looked at Jesse. "Hang on, here she is." Jesse handed her the phone. "It's for you."

Cali smiled. She knew she wouldn't be able to get on the plane without her dad calling to give her a lecture. "Hey, I'm just getting ready to board. Are you guys home yet?"

"I know you probably hate me but I couldn't let you leave without talking to you."

Cali almost dropped the phone in disbelief. "Chase?" She looked at Jesse with confusion.

"I had to let you know that I was sorry about what happened."

Cali sighed. "It's okay. I don't blame you. You couldn't have known that they would do that."

"Well, actually I'm sorry for something else."

"What?"

"For something I didn't do."

"What?" The phone went dead. "Hello?" Cali looked at Jesse. "Your phone just went dead." Someone grabbed her from behind.

She turned around and came face to face with Chase. "Chase? What are you doing here?"

"I didn't want to be with you because I didn't want to hurt you." He glanced at Jesse and then looked at her. "Someone told me that the only way I could hurt you would be to push you away."

Cali glanced at Jesse. "I don't understand. You told him to come here?"

"A lot of people told me to come here."

"I'm sorry, Chase, but I can't stay." Cali sighed. "I'm not supposed to be here anymore."

"I've already spun your life upside down. I couldn't ask for you to change anything more. I came to tell you that...I love you."

Cali smiled. "I love you too."

"I'm sorry it took me so long to realize it but if you're willing to be patient I'd like to make this work."

"Chase, I'm getting ready to fly to the other side of the world. I can't ask you to start a relationship with me." Cali shook her head. "You are the one who said that it wouldn't work."

"It wouldn't. It would be way too hard to be that far away from you." Chase pulled tickets out of his pocket. "Would it change your mind if I came with you?" Cali stared at him not sure what to reply. "There's nothing for me if I stay here."

Cali threw her arms around his neck and kissed him. Chase wrapped his arms around her and buried his head in her soft hair. "I don't mean to interrupt your happy moment but if you guys don't get moving you're going to miss your flight."

"How did you know where to go?"

"Chase's grandpa came to see me at the hotel a couple days ago when you were touching up the nursery. We had a nice long talk and now we're here."

Cali looked at Chase. She knew how hard it was to move away from your home. "Are you sure you want to do this? Just leave everything?"

"I'm not leaving everything." He grabbed her hand. "It's a long flight right? I'm sure you'll have plenty of time to convince me how great Australia is."

***

Chapter 10

Jesse sat down at the table and looked at the envelope. Cali had been promising to send pictures. He opened the envelope and unfolded the letter:

Dear Jesse,
I hope that all is going well in California. Things are going wonderful here. I think that Chase has finally got the hang of surfing. Last month, he went with Dad to India and helped build three churches. He's now attending classes at the Bible college in Sydney and he's really enjoying it. I miss Mom and Dad but the classes are only supposed to last four months so I guess I can live with it.
I can't believe that it's already been a year since I've seen you. I enclosed some pictures so you can see Chase's new hairdo. You'd be proud of him. He's really starting to look like a surfer. He's gone surfing almost every day since

we got to Sydney and I'm seriously ready to haul off and hurt him. He doesn't understand that it's no fun to watch him.

We're planning a trip back to California sometime this summer. Tell Grandpa to make sure he's kicked you out by then. Until then, be blessed and surf hard!

Miss you much! Love,

Chase and Cali Laney (and baby)

P.S. Chase said to tell Axel that running out in the middle of the night to find a restaurant that is open is horrible.

Jesse smiled and looked at the pictures. Chase's black hair was insanely curly and hanging just below his ears. Cali looked like she had stuffed a basketball under her shirt. Axel walked in the front door. "Chase just called. Cali went into labor an hour ago."

Jesse handed him the pictures. "Well, that's a good thing for her. I don't think her stomach would be able to stretch anymore."

"Are you going to be sticking around for dinner?" Victor asked Axel.

"No, David's already pissed that I've been over here as much as I have." Axel handed the pictures back to Jesse. "I came over to let you know that I finished painting the bedrooms."

"I really appreciate you helping. The doctor said

that I should have full mobility back in a couple months." Jesse looked down at the brace on his wrist.

"I don't think Victor would have let me get away without helping you."

***

About the Author

Nicole Donoho is twenty-one and the oldest of six children. She was born in Iowa and has lived in several of the eastern states. Currently, she lives with her husband, Jacob, in Arkansas. She loves to write because it opens up a door for others to dream and experience new things. She also enjoys writing children's books for her siblings and skits for her family's puppet ministry.

Printed in the United States
71415LV00001B/310-381